To my mother.
V.T.

Thank you, thank you, thank you, a thousand times and again
thank you to Alexis, Bâ-Lé, Carine, Clément, Damien, Élodie, Élise,
Emeline, Éric, Frédéric, Inès, Julien, Ludovic, Marietta, Olivier,
Romain, and Vincent!
V.T.

Published in 2009 by Windmill Books, LLC
303 Park Avenue South Suite # 1280, New York, NY 10010-3657

Adaptations to North American edition © 2009 Windmill Books
Copyright © 2006 Editions Milan, 300 rue Léon Joulin - 31101 Toulouse Cedex 9, France.

CREDITS:
Author: Amélie Sarn
Illustrator: Virgile Trouillot
A concept by Frédéric Puech and Virgile Trouillot based on an idea from Jean de Loriol.
Copyright © PLANETNEMO

Publisher Cataloging Information

Sarn, Amélie
        The audition / Amélie Sarn ; illustrations by Virgile Trouillot.
                p. cm. – (Groove High)
        Summary: Zoe and her best friend Victoria must overcome stage fright and strong competition as they try out for Groove High, the prestigious resident dance school.
        ISBN 978-1-60754-203-2. – ISBN 978-1-60754-204-9 (pbk.)
ISBN 978-1-60754-205-6 (6-pack)
        1. Dance schools—Juvenile fiction   2. Boarding schools—Juvenile fiction   3. Dancers—Juvenile fiction   [1. Dance schools—Fiction   2. Dancers—Fiction   3. Boarding schools—Fiction   4. Schools—Fiction   5. Friendship—Fiction]   I. Trouillot, Virgile   II. Title   III. Series
        [Fic]—dc22

Manufactured in the United States of America

Amélie Sarn

Illustrations by Virgile Trouillot

Skyview Books

an imprint of

WINDMILL
BOOKS
New York

Me: I'm Zoe. I'm 14 years old, and I'm living my dream: going to Groove High to become a choreographer

Vic: My best friend. Beautiful, blonde, always on the cutting edge of fashion, and fun to be around.

Lena: Athletic, rebellious, also very disorganized! Paco, her troublesome chameleon, is always in her pocket.

Tom: Very cool but very clumsy. He is crazy in love with Vic, who is not interested in him at all.

Ed: A little cold and mysterious at first glance but actually a very nice guy and a fabulous dancer!

Iris Berrens: The founder of Groove High. A legendary dancer—very intimidating.

Luke : Kim's drop-dead-gorgeous brother. Vic definitely has a crush on him.

ST4BLEE R

Table of Contents

Stage Fright

"**H**ow's it going, Vic?"

"Super, you?"

"Super!"

"You're not nervous?"

"No, not at all. You?"

"Me neither."

Of course, we are both liars! Vic does not stop moving a wisp of hair behind her ear. She always does that when she is nervous. And I should know. Victoria and I have known each other since we were seven! At the Marie Court School of Ballet, we were inseparable: Vic and Zoe, the eternal duo! And Vic did exactly the same gesture back then. I used to see her slip the same piece of hair behind her ear when it was there already, whenever she passed that cutie, Arnold, in the halls.

I have such a weight in my stomach that I feel like I swallowed a rock, and I have to grip my hands on my knees to prevent them from shaking. But aside from that, I'm fine. Super! Stage fright? Never heard of it! Pffff!

Around us, a dozen girls and boys are sitting on chairs. They arrive two or three at a time and talk to hide their fear. If I'm not chosen, I . . . I . . . don't know what I'll do! Last month, I didn't get into the Kauffman Academy. They didn't even tell me why. I thought that the world was collapsing around me. Fortunately, Vic was there. Otherwise, I would probably still be crying. Since I was five, Philippe Kauffman, the director of the Kauffman Academy, has been my absolute idol.

This man is a dance genius. The best choreographer in the world. A magician! I don't know if you've had the opportunity to see one of his ballets, but each one is new and breathtaking. Philippe Kauffman reinvents the art of dance. He gives it a deep soul and light, he . . . Anyway, I get worked up about him, and I have to get over it. I have not been accepted, and that's that.

I will give it my all to be accepted into Groove High! I have already passed the first step. Today's the big decision. Groove High is an excellent school too. Even if Philippe Kauffman does not teach there.

And you know, the history of this school is so romantic! You surely remember the events that made all the newspapers, about ten years ago. "Alexx Berrens, virtuoso choreographer, dies in a motorcycle accident," "Ballerina Iris Berrens abandons her career in full flight," "After the huge success of the musical *Dancin' Lady*, tragedy breaks apart the famous couple," etc.

At the time, I was too young to read the newspapers of course, but for all of you who are very interested in dance, the history of Alexx and Iris Berrens is a romance as heartbreaking as Romeo and Juliet.

Now . . . here, two years after the death of her husband, Iris Berrens created this school. Famous dancers Mila Kanubitsch, Pietro Sanpiero, Sandy Olive Tree, and some other stars came out of it . . . it's very well known!

"Did you see the girl who just arrived?" murmurs Vic.

I turn my head. I recognize her right away. I had spotted her at the first audition. She is so lucky. Tall, thin, jet-black hair, almond-shaped eyes, a perfect nose, a panther gait, and clothes that Vic would kill for . . . the total package!

"I LOVE her dress," mumbles Vic. "I am sure that it comes from Dori, the top Parisian designer. I saw it in *Fashion*!"

What can I say? *Fashion* is Vic's favorite magazine. She reads it almost exclusively! She treats it like a reference book for life. Vic and I, and everyone waiting, are dressed to dance. Everyone has big sweaters thrown on over tights and leotards. There's no time to change into street clothes before or after our big audition. In her short fuchsia pink dress and cropped jean jacket with embroidery, the new arrival manages to look cool.

"And her bag is amazing!" adds Vic, looking jealously at the trendy piece.

What I notice is that this girl is all alone and that she sits on a chair without looking at anyone. She is as shy and anxious as the rest of us about the audition. I don't know about you, but it makes me feel better, that a person like that, who seems to have it all and be so together, is really just like the rest of us underneath. I bet that her sign is Pisces. She is a typical Pisces—a cold appearance outside, and bubbly emotions on the inside. I get up.

"Where are you going? asks Vic.

"To say hi to the newcomer."

"Why?"

"Because she is all alone!"

Vic rolls her eyes. She knows me too well. She knows that it's not just that I want to welcome the new girl . . . I am extremely curious. I give Vic a wink and head toward the new arrival.

"Hi!"

She scarcely turns her head toward me, pinches her lips, slowly lifts her eyelids, and raises her eyebrows in a circular arch. She looks me up and down. And does not reply.

"Uhh, uh, hi," I stutter.

"Hello."

"My . . . my name is Zoe. I guess you came for the audition?"

The girl's look is glacial. I am now completely certain; there is no doubt: she is a Pisces! I give a slight cough before continuing.

"Yes, of course you're here for the audition. I'm being stupid. We are all here for the audition . . . uhh . . ."

I feel like I'm putting my foot in my mouth.

I try again. "Uhh . . . what's your name? I'm Zoe."

"You already said that," the girl says coldly.

Hmm, maybe I made a mistake. Perhaps she is not shy and nervous after all.

The double doors open and two girls walk toward me. Okay, more precisely, they walk toward the new girl. They are red and breathless. One of them carries a pink leotard. The other holds matching shoes.

"Here they are, Kim, we have it," cries the first one.

"We had trouble finding it this late," calls the second one as if she had won a medal at the Olympic Games.

"Show me!" Kim—since that must be her name—commands.

Kim gestures to dismiss me. A simple flick of the wrist, very elegant. Just like that: I'm dismissed. This girl is something else. She definitely believes she is queen of the world.

One of her friends puts a small package of paper on her knees. Kim opens it delicately . . . sushi! The package contains sushi. No peanut butter sandwich for this royalty.

"These are not my favorite," groans Her Majesty Kim. "You know that, Angie. I gave you a list the last time."

The eyes of the eager-to-please Angie widen. She turns pale.

"I know, Kim, but it's all there was and Clarisse," she pleads, referring to her nervous helper, "said that you would . . ."

I shake my head. I've seen enough, heard enough. I'm convinced. I don't know whether she's a Pisces or not, but this Kim is trouble!

I am about to return to Vic when a loud noise startles me. The door bursts open and a boy on roller skates clatters into the corridor. Everyone forgets to be nervous for a second and turns to look. He reels with his arms flailing, covers his eyes, and falls . . . right on Kim and her sushi!

Craaaaashhhh!

"Eeeeyyyhhh!" yells the queen, pushing the fallen skater off her lap and ruined lunch.

I can't help myself and burst out laughing.

Raw fish and rice are arranged on the boy's face like a constellation. Kim's beautiful outfit is ruined. Angie and Clarisse have sheepish expressions, and I just can't stop laughing at the scene.

The boy manages to regain his balance on his roller skates, as he stammers apologetically:

"Uhh . . . sorry . . . I guess . . . my roller skates . . . they . . . uhhh . . . sorry! I'm Tom!"

Chapter 2

Two Dramatic Entrances

Red as a tomato from his embarrassing entrance, Tom tries to remove the residue of sushi from his cheeks and his forehead. It is funny. His hair is in a small ridiculous pony tail, and he is draped in an immense sweatshirt that could probably fit four of him. Kim gets up and stares daggers at him. I would not be surprised if she began to roar and jump on the poor guy, like a lioness with her claws out! Or if she put herself in a kung-fu position and used two or three well-placed blows to transform him into sushi! But, without a word, her chin raised high, Her Majesty Kim directs herself toward the ladies' room. She is quickly followed by her doting groupies, Angie and Clarisse. Poor Tom, looking like he wants to disappear, sheepishly searches for a chair. All eyes are on him. All of a sudden, he turns an even deeper shade of red than before. Scarlet! Crimson! I raise my eyebrows when I see the cause. He has just noticed Vic. He can't stop staring at her.

Vic is completely unaware of his adoration. Her expression is so disapproving anyone can see that she thinks this boy is ridiculous. I know Vic as well as my own family, and he's not her type at all! Oblivious to all of this, Tom heads toward Vic. He sees my empty chair, which is next to Vic's. He must think it is free. I am about to intervene and save him from further humiliation, when the door to the corridor swings open.

All eyes turn toward the man who comes through the door. The door! My heart beats faster. That door leads to the audition room. What happens behind that door will decide our fate. I know it. Everyone in this hall is thinking the same thought.

The man who has just entered is fantastic. He seems magical. He has big, square shoulders, black hair, skin with a magnificent clear chocolate tint, and soft but dark eyes.

"Young people, I wish you all welcome," says the man, smiling.

He has very white teeth and a magnetic smile.

"Let me introduce myself. My name is Khan. Actually, that's my nickname but I will spare you trying to pronounce my actual name, which contains no fewer than 48 letters. So, you can just remember 'Khan.'

"I am the yoga teacher at this school, and I hope that you will all succeed at the audition, so I'll have an opportunity to teach you the beautiful practice of yoga."

Yoga! If I get into Groove High, yoga will definitely be my favorite class! Okay, I've actually never done yoga but, now that I've seen the mesmerizing Khan, I'm sure it will be my favorite class!

"Iris Berrens, Groove High's founder and director, organizes this audition every year. If you are here, you know that you have already made the first cut. Today, you will dance in front of the third-year students, who will help us to evaluate your technique, the originality of your choreography, and your potential for succeeding at Groove High."

Khan widens his smile, but this time, his sweet voice is not enough to distract me from what he is saying. I can't believe other students are going to judge my audition. The idea that a girl like Her Majesty Kim is going to dissect and critique my performance gives me chills. I am ready to bet my first tutu that she is not the indulgent type! Just then, the queen of sushi comes out of the restroom, flanked by her devoted followers. She has transformed. Now she's sporting a fuchsia tank top and pale pink shorts. Somehow, she even managed to produce a coordinated bag.

Kim nods to Khan who returns a nod to her. She knows the yoga teacher! Bad luck.

"Well, auditioners," resumes Khan, "it is time to go. Good luck to all. Take some deep breaths and try to relax as much as possible."

The yoga teacher steps aside so we can enter the audition room. Before the rest of us have had a chance to move, Kim advances, signals to her friends to follow her, and enters the room first.

I have not seen Vic approach me. She takes my hand in hers. I am so glad she is here. We're always there for each other. No matter what happens at today's audition, we'll be ourselves and hope for the best. We head for the door together.

Chapter 3

Zoe's Strategy

The audition room is pretty spectacular. It's very classical, with a stage and armchairs in red velvet. The third-year students sit on the armchairs, whispering among themselves. Khan has us sign our names on a sheet of paper. We will audition as our names are called.

A tall, very thin woman, with her hands folded behind her back, stands on the stage. Her hair is pulled up in a tight bun. She carries a leotard and a chiffon skirt. She does not smile. Despite her formal appearance, her movements are extremely graceful. Khan sits in the first row, but I am no longer distracted by him. Iris Berrens—the woman on the stage—is terribly intimidating, and commands my full attention.

I peek at Vic, who is staring at Iris with an air of devotion. I am not surprised. Vic's favorite movie is

Dancin' Lady, the musical drama in which Iris Berrens is the heroine. Vic can watch that movie ten times in one day. And each time she watches the tragic ending, she is in tears. In spite of her weakness for that particular movie, Vic is not usually one to wear her heart on her sleeve. Vic is a Taurus. Actually her birthday puts her between a Taurus and a Gemini. You can imagine the mixture, if you're into astrology like me. It's an explosive combination!

But back to Iris Berrens. In spite of a very intense twelve-year career, Iris still looks youthful in many ways. I just wish a smile would lighten her austere appearance.

"Young people," begins Iris Berrens, "before we review the rules of the audition, I want you to understand what kind of school you may be about to enter. If you are here, you have a passion: dancing. You also have a goal, a dream: you want to live this passion. Well, remember that in my school, this dream is paid in one currency: hard work! Your work!" After a calculated pause, Iris Berrens adds: "If any one does not feel capable, has self-doubts, is too frightened, or not ready to give all your energy for this school, then leave now. It will save you a great deal of wasted time."

A heavy silence follows this announcement, which sounds more like a war declaration. If that was Iris Berrens's effort to put us at ease, it didn't work. In my heart, I don't think it is her intention to scare us. As her piercing gaze sweeps across the semi-darkened room, I sense that she is trying to guess which of us will crack, who might be too lazy to succeed, or who will try, but fold under the pressure. All of us hold ourselves as tall as we can. Even if I had wanted to get up and run out of there, which is not the case, I assure you, I would not have dared to move an eyelash! There is something about Iris Berrens that keeps you frozen in place.

Iris Berrens begins again. "This is the audition sequence. We will call the first three of you. While one student auditions, the next has ten minutes to warm up in the rehearsal room. When you audition, you will have to execute a free variation of classical dance for two minutes and thirty seconds on an excerpt of Swan Lake. For the second part, you have options. You may choose from contemporary dance, acrobatic dance, modern jazz, hip-hop, or capoeira. The stage is forty feet across and twenty-five feet deep, which should allow you to move and express yourself freely. Now, it's up to you."

Iris Berrens prepares to descend from the stage, but suddenly she has an idea.

"I forgot, all those not in proper dress will be eliminated; a leotard and tights are preferred. Loose or flowing clothing is forbidden. Of course, pointe shoes are required for the classical part!"

Next to me, Tom, in his baggy sweatshirt, chews his nails nervously. Iris Berrens descends off the stage and Khan replaces her immediately. He holds a card in his hand.

"I call Miss Kimberley Vandenberg. Miss Cindy Roberts, you will begin your warm up as soon as Miss Vandenberg enters the stage. Mr. Tom Muller will be next. I will call the others as we go along."

Kim, always majestic, detaches herself from the group. Evidently, as if they can't prevent themselves, Clarisse and Angie start to get up to follow her backstage. Kim whistles to them—I swear to you, when she whistles, I hear rattles that belong to a rattlesnake—to direct them to remain in their seats.

Before climbing onstage, she turns toward the audience and nods to a third year student. Obviously, this girl knows everyone here! I watch him return the look and nod back. I inhale sharply. What a handsome hunk! Even though he's sitting down, I can tell that the third-year boy is tall and muscular. He has perfectly groomed black hair and clear skin. He leans back nonchalantly in his chair, his arm resting on the chair next to him. The girl in the chair looks tense. She might be anxious about the audi-

tion, but she probably is breathless just to be sitting next to this guy. He's so relaxed. A typical Don Juan! If this is Kim's boyfriend, she must be seething that he's sitting with his arm nearly touching the girl next to him. She's blonde with a figure like a fashion model. That irritates me! I hate it when these playboys just look at a girl's appearance with no interest in her personality or intelligence. Kim's expression is just as icy and superior as ever as she climbs the stairs to the stage and disappears behind the curtains. Now I suspect that the guy is not her boyfriend.

I try to breathe calmly and not be nervous. I remind myself that I've been preparing for months. My dancing is not technically perfect, but I'm confident of the originality of my choreography. So, I'm betting I'll win this audition on that. Now that I have seen and heard Iris Berrens, I begin to regret this strategy. Her late husband, Alexx Berrens, choreographed all the shows in which she danced, and his pieces were so innovative and original that I wanted to impress her with those qualities. Now, I realize that a lot can change in twelve years. Maybe, being without her husband, some of her love for originality and creativity has been lost. After all, she's been in the classical, academic world for years now. I wonder if it's all over for me before my audition starts. I'm sure she won't like my style. I'll wind up back at the Marie Court School of Ballet. I'll never be famous!

"Zoe! Zoe! You okay? "

I raise my eyes toward Vic.

"Uh . . . yes, yes, I'm fine . . ."

"You look a little upset," murmurs my friend. "Don't tell me it's because of that show-off Kimberley?"

I shrug my shoulders.

"No, that isn't it. Not really. It's just that my stomach is all tied up in knots. And it just keeps getting worse now that I know I'll be dancing in front of the third years, including Kim's friend . . . that playboy guy and the girl who looks like a model. I'm just feeling stressed."

"Iris Berrens is inspiring, right?" demands Vic, forcing me to forget my nervousness.

"Uh . . . yes, yes . . ." I hesitate a second before posing my next question, but then I remind myself that Vic is my best friend. I can ask her anything.

"Tell me, Vic . . ."

"What?"

"Do you think . . ." I take a shaky breath. "Do you think that my figure is okay?"

Vic sighs.

"Don't start that again! We've talked about that ten times. You're a knock-out. And you're not here to be judged on your figure. You're here to be judged on your dancing."

"It's easy for you to say that, since you look like a model! You're so . . ."

"Hi!" a voice interrupts our quiet moment.

We look up at the grinning boy who has just greeted us. It's Tom, the crazy skater, who has eyes only for Vic. He's smitten!

On Stage

While fixated on Vic, Tom whispers:

"Hi, I'm Tom."

Vic raises an eyebrow.

"Yes, we know," I say. "We saw your big entrance!"

Tom blushes. I giggle. I can tell he's one of those people who blushes easily. He starts to turn tomato-red again.

"Oh, yeah. The wheels kind of got the better of me."

I shake my head.

"Forget it. I'm Zoe and this is my best friend, Vic."

"I see—Vic." He says her name admiringly.

I knew it! The boy has fallen head over heels for Vic. Oh, the poor thing!

Tom blinks. Then, hopelessly out of control, his feelings spill out.

"Vic, I bet you're a great dancer. You're wonderful!"

Vic does not respond. Tom is oblivious and continues.

"I . . . would you . . . would you want to go out with me sometime?"

Vic opens her mouth to protest, as Tom chatters on about a possible date.

"Please, there's an audition behind you!" a voice says sternly.

Iris Berrens directs her words to us. Now, it's my turn to blush. I lower my head. This is really not the time to be noticed. At least not in this way.

"Be quiet," Vic whispers angrily to her never-will-be boyfriend. "We don't want to get in trouble!"

Tom does not need to be told twice. The curtain crashes down on his romantic overture. Sweet guy. And a funny one. Kind of clumsy and awkward, but cute in a way. Maybe Vic will see his potential.

Music begins to play and I turn my head. Kim makes her entrance. She has left her long black hair down. Delicately circling her arms, she glides to the middle of the stage. She is . . . feline. No, it is not possible. This girl cannot be beautiful, rich, AND talented!

After dancing, she is very confident among us mere mortals, and she can't resist exchanging another nod with the third year guy, whose arm is now touching the girl next to him. Near Tom, a girl with a bandana on her head, leans toward Kim and whispers:

"Your audition was incredible. You're a great dancer."

Kim looks regally around at the rest of us, who are still nervously waiting our turns to take the stage. Then she takes a seat between her two groupies, who lavish her with praise for her flawless audition. She accepts this admiration, and then, in a smooth voice, but loud enough for everyone to hear, offers her opinion of another auditioner.

"I saw the next girl warming up," Kim sneers. "She is about as graceful as a hippo! If she is chosen, this school does not deserve its reputation!"

Beautiful, rich, and talented? Yes, and cruel.

Next to me, Vic shakes her head. No chance that my Taurus friend will allow this high-and-mighty girl to be so rude. Very quietly, without raising her voice, but commanding attention, as only she can, Vic addresses Kim.

"You're right, this school is not a zoo. But you'd fit right in if it were, since you've just given us a perfect impression of a vicious snake."

Kim grits her teeth at Vic's sharp retort, and silently returns her a scathing look. Vic's the champion of putting people in their place, but only when they need it. Vic never does it maliciously, but this girl deserved it.

It's Tom's turn to go backstage. I wait impatiently for his performance. Could be interesting. It's already off to a silly start. He forgot to take off his skates, and he's skating toward the stage. Or trying to. When he rolls past Kim, she proves how snakey she can be by sticking her foot out. Tom falls on his face. Every third year bursts out laughing.

"Kindly remove your skates, Mr. Muller," Iris Berrens sighs.

Needless to say, Tom is red as a lobster. Distracted by the director's tone, Tom doesn't have a moment to deal with Kim. He struggles with the straps on his skates. Finally, he manages to remove them, but things don't get much better. Everyone can see his crazy yellow socks now. He drops his skates, leaving them right in front of Kim, who bends down to push them aside.

Vic grins. A chance to get back at Kim!

"How sweet of you to offer to take care of your buddy's skates," Vic says, in a loud, cheery voice. "You're such a loyal friend of Tom's!"

The auditioners look more interested now. Kim tries to remain cool and ignore the skates that announce her friendship with Tom.

While Tom disappears backstage, Cindy Roberts enters the scene. Kim was wrong to criticize Cindy. She dances well. She chose modern jazz and a rather

pretty swing free variation. Her audition goes smoothly. Cindy finishes her performance and exits the stage. Khan rises and calls a name.

"Edward Kauffman can warm up!"

My ears prick up like a cat's. Edward Kauffman? Is it possible that this boy is related to Philippe Kauffman, my dance hero? It can't be. If Philippe Kauffman, the talented, amazing Philippe Kauffman had a son, I would know. I read all the gossip magazines that I come by. The exploits of Philippe Kauffman are described in great detail, but I've never read about a son. And, of course, it's ridiculous. If the choreographer Philippe Kauffman had a son, why would he apply to Groove High? Why wouldn't he attend the school his father runs?

A boy with dark brown hair, who's been sitting quietly in the back of the room, stands. Without looking at anyone, he climbs on stage. He looks classic, in a white shirt and V-neck sweater vest.

I can't believe it. I am certain he is related to the famous choreographer. I have dozens of photos of Philippe Kauffman hanging on the walls of my room, and this boy is his mirror image.

Tom's audition didn't go too badly. He certainly showed great originality in his theatrical expression. He chose hip-hop and seemed to be doing some kind of jungle-animal theme. It was different from any dance I'd ever seen, but not bad at all.

As soon as Tom leaves the stage, he is replaced by the mysterious Edward Kauffman who took barely any time to warm up.

From his first step, I am moved. Edward dances as if he is reciting a poem through movement. He is bewitching. His steps and gestures are quiet and re-fined. The more I watch, the more I am sure that this boy has nothing in common with the flashy Philippe Kauffman, who is known for his flamboyant dance style.

Edward finishes his classical audition and goes imediately into his free variation. This next piece is in modern jazz style, like Cindy's performance. It's amazing how he switches from one genre to another so effortlessly. His jazz has a completely different feel to it.

We are so impressed that we don't see it coming. As he is pre-paring to make a jump, Edward Kauffman . . . falls hard on the floor of the stage.

Chapter 5

More Waiting

I let out a cry. Iris Berrens and Khan rush to the stage, joined by the third years who are audition judges. I put my hand on my mouth. Edward Kauffman is on the ground, two tight fists to his chest, as if he's having trouble breathing. Mrs. Berrens and Khan hover over him nervously as he recovers from having the wind knocked out of him.

Khan looks at the rest of us. "We will take a break before continuing the audition. Please go to the warm-up room off the hallway and use it to practice while you're waiting."

We go back to the hallway, buzzing about the unexpected turn of events in Edward Kauffman's audition.

"What happened?"

"I don't understand, everything was fine and then,

boom, he's on the ground."

"The boy's a wimp," Kim's voice rises above the crowd. "He got too ambitious with his choreography. He shouldn't have tried to do more than he could handle."

"Gee, Kim, are you always so empathetic?" asks the girl with the bandana on her head.

Kim does not bother to answer. The girl in the bandana shrugs and approaches Vic and me.

"Hi, my name is Lena."

"Hi, I'm Zoe and this is Vic," I offer.

"This snake here, who keeps spitting her venom, do you know her?" Lena asks, nodding toward Kim.

I shrug.

"I know her name is Kim and I plan to steer clear of her."

"I think that's a good call," Lena agrees. "I hope I get into Groove High. This school has such a good reputation, and it's so cool that it's a boarding school!

I'd love to live away from home."

Like many major schools of dance, Groove High wants students to live on-site and fully committed to the program. The letter inviting us to today's audition informed us that students who are selected must plan to stay for three days. In other words, the dance audition is just the first step. Students who are selected must also spend three days proving to Iris Berrens that they have all the other qualities that it takes to be a student at Groove High. You should have seen Mom at the train station when she dropped Vic and me off for the ride to Groove High. Three days without her baby daughter. You would have thought I was going to the moon!

"Do you like the idea of a boarding school?" I ask Lena.

"Are you kidding? Anything that gives me a little space from my parents sounds good to me!"

I look around me happily. The school really is wonderful. The amphitheater is vast and decorated with beautiful paintings of famous dances and dancers. The large windows bring in a warm light, which shines on the fascinating collection of dance gear, costumes, and equipment. Some doors along the hallway are left ajar, and you can see dressing rooms for star dancers, with large mirrors ringed by bright lights.

"It's amazing, isn't it?" Lena marvels. I nod.

"That's the warm-up room!" Kim announces authoritatively, pointing to a mirror-filled studio.

Kim enters and takes a moment to admire her reflection in the room full of mirrors before going to a ballet barre to stretch. I hate to admit it since she's so mean, but she really is a pretty girl. Seeing her reflection in all the floor-to-ceiling mirrors confirms that opinion.

I head over to an empty space at a barre, reminding myself that the glorious Khan suggested we use this break to practice. I wonder where Vic has gotten to, when I hear her firm voice.

"I already told you that I don't want to go out with you!" Vic is trying to make her complete lack of interest in Tom clear, but this extremely persistent and optimistic guy will not take no for an answer. Maybe I should tell hopeless Tom that Vic is a Taurus and that she's stubborn and unlikely to change her mind.

"Look, the two klutzes have found each other!" Kim teases, as she watches Tom's one-sided adoration and Vic's unsuccessful efforts to get rid of him.

"So, what do you like more about him?" Kim chortles, "his terrible sense of fashion, or his terrible dancing?"

"Say, Madame Witch, why don't you take a bite of your own poison apple and leave him alone?" Vic shouts to Kim.

Once again, Vic manages to leave Kim speechless,

or at least stewing in silence. Tom, on the other hand, is delighted that Vic stood up for him. It's clear from the goofy expression on his face that he's about to pledge his lifelong gratitude to her. But before he has a chance to drop on bended knee, Kim shrieks with delight.

She rushes across the dance studio to greet the handsome third year who'd nodded to her when she took the stage for her audition. He's just entered the room with his stunning companion.

"Hey, little sister," he says in a pompous tone. "I want you to meet Anita."

So he's her brother! That's the connection. Makes sense that they're family. He has the same unattractive habit of looking people up and down disapprovingly.

Without taking a look at the glamorous Anita, Kim grabs her brother's arm. "Tell me, Luke," she says with a voice loud enough for everyone to hear. (Does she really think everyone always wants to hear everything she has to say?) "You're in charge of the Capoeira Club at school, right?"

Luke frees his arm from his sister and takes his girlfriend, Anita's, hand in his again. Anita can't seem to stop smiling foolishly at Luke.

I decide not to give these people any more of my attention. I find Lena. She is deep in concentration, stretching her athletic limbs. I start bending and stretching, loosening up my tight muscles.

Lena exhales. "Gosh, that guy is some flirt! Checking everyone out while he's parading his picture-perfect girlfriend around. Bet he's dating her for her brains, huh?"

Lena and I understand each other perfectly. Unfortunately, at the same time, I catch sight of my image in the mirror and I sigh, disappointed with my reflection.

"Why don't you introduce me to your friends?" Luke says suddenly to his sister. "Did you all get introduced before the audition started?"

Her friends?! His sister probably doesn't even know what that word means! I look back to Lena. I'm still curious about Edward Kauffman.

"Lena, what about the boy who fell? Edward Kauffman. Do you know who he is?"

Lena gives me a wide-eyed stare.

"How could I not? He is the son of Philippe Kauffman! Haven't you ever heard of Philippe Kauffman?"

While Lena and discuss the Kauffman connection, Kim is giving Luke a who's who.

"You already know Angie and Clarisse?" Kim says, gesturing to her personal fan club.

"Oh, yes, of course. Hello, clones!" Luke says.

I have to admit that makes me chuckle to myself, even if I'm trying to pay attention to what Lena's saying.

Angie and Clarisse aren't daunted by Luke's sarcasm. "Hi, Luke," they say in unison, batting their eyes.

On my other side, I can't believe what I'm hearing from Lena. How could I miss the existence of Philippe Kauffman's son? But what about the media? How did they miss this vital piece of information?

"Are you sure?" I ask Lena.

"Yes, I am sure." she says.

This is crazy! Not only does Philippe Kauffman

have a son, but the son is my age! And better yet: I have seen him! In the flesh! The son of my idol! My jaw drops open in disbelief.

"Zoe, shut your mouth!" Lena whispers to me.

I snap my mouth closed. Just in time. The flirty Luke is coming right toward me. What does he want with me? Never mind, he stops in the middle of the studio.

"Hello, everybody," he says smoothly. "Great job to those of you who have already presented, and good luck to the rest of you. I am sure you heard what Khan said before. The most important thing for your audition is to remain focused and relaxed."

Who does he think he is? I roll my eyes. He's trying to be so smart and wise, but nobody's buying it! Okay, so he's a third year at Groove High, but he still doesn't know everything. He's still a student, just like us—at least, just like all of us want to be. Now where is Vic, again? I keep losing her. Oh, there she is! She is leaning against an exercise barre, and I can't believe my eyes, but the unflappable Vic is staring at Luke. She looks like a love-struck zombie.

"You must be careful to keep your back straight when you're in that position!" a voice says, startling me. It's Luke. He's chosen to come over to me to give me advice.

"Close your mouth, Zoe," says Lena again.

I snap my mouth shut automatically, and at the same time mechanically straighten my back. I just did it by instinct. I wasn't trying to follow this know-it-all's advice. I swear. I have nothing to learn from this kind of show-off.

"Yes, that's better, Carrot Top!"

Carrot Top! I'm not making this up. He called me Carrot Top in front of everyone! I'm desperate to think of a clever comeback. But I'm not Vic. I'm not witty when I need to be. Speaking of Vic, why didn't she come to my defense with one of her smart-aleck comments? It's not like her to leave me hanging.

"Above all, remember," says Luke to the group, "concentrate and stay relaxed. That's how you'll ace this audition."

With these words, he turns and leaves, with the vapid Anita still clinging to his arm.

I'm still reeling from the Carrot Top remark. All this because my hair is a little red. Actually, it's not red. According to the bottle I got my highlights from, it's strawberry blonde. I spot Vic, but before I can even ask why she let this conceited guy get away with insulting me, Vic opens her mouth and exhales ecstatically.

"He is gorgeous, isn't he, Zoe?"

Oh, no! Not you, too, Vic! She's just as goofy about Luke as Tom is about her.

Chapter
6

Insecurity and Betrayal

Concentrate and stay relaxed! Like that's easy advice to follow when our futures are at stake! And with everything that's happened. First, I am terribly angry with Vic. She completely dropped the ball. I had to get away so as not to say anything I'd regret. I can't believe she likes a guy who humiliated me in public. That's not what a friend should do. Let alone a best friend. And that's not all. It feels like the whole audition is turning into a nightmare.

First, a dancer falls onstage. Everyone knows that's bad luck. I am not particularly superstitious, but, for dancers, that's like a mirror breaking. Then there's this high-and-mighty Kim making everyone feel more insecure than we already do; Kim's stuck-on-himself brother Luke running around calling me Carrot Top isn't helping either; and, on top of it, I can't believe that my idol, Philippe Kauffman, who

I pride myself on knowing everything about, has a son my age—and I didn't realize it! And, worst of all, seeing Luke's voluptuous girlfriend and some of these other girls is just reminding me how pitiful my own figure is.

Just as I finish my laundry list of disasters at this audition, Tom collapses on the floor in front of me. In a high-pitched, voice, he says "Look at me everybody, even in a pile on the floor, I'm the most beautiful and talented dancer at the audition!"

I can't help but laugh. It's a perfect imitation of snooty Kim. This Tom is beginning to grow on me.

Then Khan comes

in to announce that Edward Kauffman, the dancer who collapsed onstage, just fainted, probably due to fatigue, but he's doing fine now. Khan says we have five minutes to warm up, then the next lineup of dancers will be Vic, Angie, and . . . me.

In twenty, twenty-five minutes, I will dance in front of conceited Luke and the other third years. I hope Luke will be able to judge my dancing and not my pathetic figure. And what about the other third years? And Khan? And Iris Berrens? What will they think of my audition? I am so nervous, I feel like running out the door.

Vic sidles over to me. She looks sheepish.

"Zoe, I'm . . ." she stammers.

Are you ready, Vic, to promise me that you do not like that stupid pretentious Luke? But I get no such assurance.

"I have to go. I'm up," she says breathlessly. "Will you come backstage to support me?"

My mouth hangs open. I can't believe it. No apology. No assurance. No, Vic is just asking me to support her. I bite the inside of my cheek—a bad habit I have when I'm feeling upset and confused.

"Come on, Zoe. You know I need you."

I look at Vic's imploring blue eyes. I can't say no to my best friend, even when she's not acting like one. And she knows it.

"Yes, of course, I'll root you on," I say.

Vic smiles at me.

"You promise, Zoe?"

"Don't worry, Vic. You know you'll always be my best friend, and I'll always support you."

I give her a hug.

"I have to go back there in two minutes," she murmurs, heading toward the door into the auditorium.

I wonder if she realizes how much she hurt my feelings. I'll have to worry about that later. I have bigger worries to face right now. How can I give the best audition of my life and impress Khan and Iris Berrens? Is there anything I can do to make myself more attractive and win the superficial Luke's vote of approval?

Maybe I should ask Lena. She seems smart and nice. Not to mention confident. Maybe she has an idea. Just as I turn to scan the room for Lena, there she is, right in front of me.

"I can't believe that Kim girl," Lena begins. "She's

quite a piece of work, don't you think?"

Of course, I nod in agreement.

"And she is so worried about how she looks, she doesn't spend any time thinking about how she acts, or makes other people feel. She probably spends half her day in front of the mirror, worrying about her appearance."

I nod weakly. I am pretty consumed with my own appearance right now, even though I know it's superficial of me.

"It kills me, that kind of girl," Lena resumes vehemently. "The kind who thinks that her appearance is the most essential thing in life! The kind who thinks the great existential questions are: Am I having a good hair day? Does my lipstick match my bag? Ridiculous! As if there aren't things a thousand times more important to worry about in life."

I agree with Lena, but right now I'm feeling too insecure to worry about being a little shallow. Still, I decide Lena may not be the right person to ask for a suggestion about how to improve my figure in a hurry.

Lena offers a sympathetic smile.

"You seem preoccupied. Is it stage fright?"

"Huh? What? No, no, I'm fine."

"Look," she continues waving toward the door, "that skater guy went to see your friend audition. He seems like he's really into her."

I nod my head. My brain is too busy to focus on Tom.

"It really made me laugh to see his wacky yellow socks before," says Lena. "And I like someone who's a free spirit like that. He doesn't care what other people think of him."

Socks! This might be the perfect solution to my problem.

"Thanks, Lena! I've got to run."

Lena looks at me, puzzled.

"What are you talking about? What are you thanking me for?"

Without knowing it, Lena has just solved my dilemma. Now, I just have to tell Vic the brilliant solution.

Oh, no, Vic! I can't believe it. I completely spaced! She's probably onstage by now, and I've totally forgotten to go backstage to cheer her on.

I start for the auditorium frantically, bumping into someone in my rush.

"Get out of my way. I have to get backstage. My friend is . . . oh, it's you."

I see the person I've bumped into is Vic. I've missed her whole audition.

She shoots me a look.

"Oh, Vic, I'm so sorry. I was . . ."

"I know where you were, Zoe," Vic interrupts in a sharp voice. "You stayed in the dance studio to chat with your new friend!"

My new friend? She must mean Lena. Is she jealous? No, that can't be the problem. Vic knows she's my best friend, that I won't let her down. Except that I have just let her down. I promised to support her during her audition, the most important moment of our lives so far, and I totally blew it.

"Well, hello, girls!" Tom interrupts to shower Vic with praise.

"You were great! You were amazing out there. Your technique was perfect. You're a shoo-in for this place."

Vic presses her lips together tightly and walks by me, heading back for the dance studio, with Tom following her, a flood of compliments pouring out. Vic does not even bother to wave Tom off. She's only got one thing on her mind, and that's how much I've disappointed her. My throat is too tight to talk. I can't even try to apologize. I've never seen her look so mad. And so hurt.

"What happened, Zoe? You look like you've just seen a ghost. Pull yourself together, you are on in five minutes."

It's Lena. She puts a comforting hand on my shoulder.

"Listen," she says with a smile, "you must not let stage fright get you down. You know you're a good

dancer. Now you just have to go out there and show other people how good you are. It's as simple as that."

As simple as that. Is she kidding me? Nothing about this audition feels simple right now.

"Are you still worrying about that stuck-up Luke teasing you and calling you Carrot Top? Forget about it. Next time I see him, I'll give him a piece of my mind."

Lena's smile is so reassuring. Now this is how a friend is supposed to act. She's taking my side against Luke, instead of looking at him with dreamy eyes and calling him gorgeous. I'm still mad at Vic for that. Then again, now I've just left her alone during her audition, when I promised I'd be there for her. How can all this be happening today of all days? But Lena's right, I've got to pull myself together. I only have a few minutes to put my plan into effect.

When I enter the dance studio, Vic does not even cast a glance in my direction. She is in a corner of the room, with her nose in her bag rummaging for something. I want to rush over to her and try to make her laugh. She always forgives me when I make her laugh. She can't help herself. But there's no time. Right now, I have to focus on my audition. I go to my bag and take out what I need and head back toward the auditorium.

"It's your turn to go, Carrot Top. Are you ready?"

It's Kim, echoing her brother Luke's cruel teasing.

"That's what you like to be called, right? Carrot Top!" Kim asks nastily.

I set my chin and clench my fists, and walk right past her without a word. This is my dream. I have to ace this audition. I can't let this snobby girl get me off track.

Catastrophe

Well, the moment is finally here. It's my turn to audition.

My palms are sweating. My stomach's in knots, but I must not let it get to me. Once, Mr. Garrison, my dance teacher at the Marie Court School of Ballet, said: "Zoe, if you want to succeed, you need to learn to control your stage fright. The fright is part of an audition as much as the dancing. Accept it. Turn the fear into energy and let it work for you instead of against you."

He was right. I have to get all this nervous energy under control and use it to fuel my performance. If only Vic were here to give me some encouragement. To reassure my that my choice to "enhance" my figure was the right one. I quickly look down at the new curve of my leotard. Okay, Groove High, here I come in all my glory. Now I'm on stage. The lights are on me. It's time to dance.

When I dance, I forget everything. Usually. But not this time. I see the severe face of Iris Berrens and, beside it, the silhouette of Khan. I want to impress them so much. I try to focus on the steps, think about my technique. Then I see Luke and his girlfriend. Are they grinning? Are they laughing at me, while I'm so vulnerable up here on stage, or is my imagination playing tricks on me? And then there are these . . . these socks! Yes, I did it! I actually stuffed a pair of socks into my bra right before I came onstage. And I'm not used to having extra weight on my chest when I dance. It's throwing off my rhythm.

But, wait, I do a pirouette, and it's perfect. Just when I think things might turn out okay, it happens. The unthinkable happens. One of the socks shifts and I suddenly have a lump in the middle of my stomach! I try to arch my back to readjust, but it only causes an even worse disaster. The other sock pops out of my leotard entirely and rolls onto the stage. This is the end of the world.

I am beet red and frozen at center stage. There's

dead silence in the auditorium. I thought everyone would burst out laughing, but this total silence is even worse. I don't know what to do. My heart is beating at a crazy pace, and my brain is racing wildly as I try to figure out what to do next. What should I do next? Run offstage and give up my dream? Keep dancing? Start to cry?

Suddenly a voice that doesn't even sound like my own speaks. It's me, but it feels like it's coming from someone else.

"Please excuse me. May I start again at the beginning?"

"Of course, miss," the response comes back. It's the voice of Iris Berrens, and it's not as harsh as I expect. It actually sounds kind.

I go back to the sidelines. Tom is there. He puts his hand on my sleeve and gives me a sympathetic smile. I fish the other sock out of my leotard, resigned to a flatter figure. Tom discreetly looks away. He really is a nice guy. But I'm not worried about nice guys like Tom or spoiled guys like Luke anymore. All I'm worried about now is that I may have blown my dream.

I won't be accepted to Groove High. I'll have to return to the ballet school near home. I'll never be a famous choreographer. Well, now I have nothing to lose. I hear my audition music starting again. I have no other choice. I'll give this performance everything I've got. Maybe I can still salvage my dignity, even if I've ruined my dream.

War, Peace, and War

And suddenly we're all back in the hallway, as if we'd never moved. As if none of us has auditioned, or embarrassed ourselves, or fainted, or disappointed friends. The audition is over. And now we're all just sitting and waiting. Waiting to learn our fate.

Lena did a great job. Her acrobatic dance was breathtaking. She looked like she was made of rubber. Me? How did my performance go after the disaster? What can I say? I did my best in my modern dance routine. I didn't make any mistakes. I felt like I was dancing for my life. But I have no illusions. Groove High's mission is to train dancers, not circus performers. And my first attempt was definitely a freak show.

Vic is sitting as far away from me as possible. It's too bad. I could really use her company right now.

My future is on the line. She doesn't have to worry. She'll be accepted. She's a great dancer, and I'm sure she did an amazing job in her audition, even if I didn't see it. What will happen when she gets into Groove High and I don't? Will that be the end of our friendship? And as if the end of my friendship with Vic wouldn't be bad enough, I'm sure the snobby Kim will get in to Groove High, too. For all her personality flaws, she really can dance.

Anyway, that's the future and I have enough to worry about in the present. I'm never going to live down the ridiculous "socks" incident. What was I thinking anyway?

At least Kim wasn't in the auditorium, but I'm sure her brother Luke will tell her all about my humiliating catastrophe. Vic wasn't there either. Maybe she'd be able to tell me it wasn't so bad if she'd seen it.

Lena, meanwhile, offered one comment: "It was very original!" I know I should try to find the humor in the situation, too, but right now I feel like the most unfortunate person on the face of the earth.

Behind the door, the famous door, Iris Berrens, Khan, Luke, Luke's girlfriend, and the other third years are deliberating. Are they laughing at me in there? Are they laughing at all of us poor souls sitting out here in the hallway, our fate hanging in the balance?

Tom sits near Vic. She skillfully ignores him. For some reason it annoys me that he doesn't even seem nervous—his knees aren't even shaking.

"Calm down," Lena sighs every five minutes.

"I am calm," I keep shooting back. But really I'm a mess.

Lena is constantly fiddling with her bag. Or more accurately, she seems to be talking to it! She opens her purse, plunges her hand in it; the bag rumbles; she closes the bag and guards it on her knees rocking back and forth . . .

Tom look over and asks, "What have you got in there?"

Lena huddles closer to her bag protectively.

"Me? Nothing. I don't have anything in my bag."

Looking down at the other end of the corridor, I see Vic tucking and re-tucking a wisp of hair behind her ear. Seeing that familiar nervous gesture makes me feel sympathetic. I get up and head toward Vic.

I'm gearing up to apologize, when Vic snaps at me,

"Are you already bored with your new best friend?"

I step back in shock. I have come to make peace, but she still wants to be at war. Fine. Two can play that game.

"No, not at all. Lena is very nice and funny, actually."

"Good for her, and I am sure she doesn't let her friends down in the most important moments of their lives either."

Ouch, that hurt.

"Maybe you're right about that. Maybe I did mess up big-time by missing your

audition, but you let me down today, too. Some strange boy we've never met before insults me, your best friend, and instead of defending me, you act like you're falling in love with him."

Vic gets up. We stand face to face.

"I don't know what you're talking about! I'm not in love with any boy and ..."

Kim is enjoying our battle. "Look at the two losers fighting," she chortles. "Perhaps Groove High has lowered its standards. Seems like they'll let anyone try out."

Vic and I both turn toward Kim.

"Who do you think you are?" I shout.

Vic yells out at the same time. "You are so full of yourself!"

Before Kim has time to respond to either one of us, a yell rips out across the hallway!

Chaos

"Aaaaaahhhhh!"

It's Tom who cried out.

"What's wrong? What happened?" I ask Tom.

"Look," says Tom, pointing to Lena.

Lena is down on the floor, on all fours, calling out in a desperate voice:

"Paco! Paco!"

Now another piercing shrink rings out. Kim has jumped up onto a chair and is screaming like she's seen a ghost.

"Help! Help!"

It's total chaos in the hallway now.

"A rat! It's a rat. I saw it!" Kim shrieks.

All the girls climb on chairs except Vic, me, and Lena . . . who runs up to Kim asking, "Where? Where did you see it?"

"It was right by my feet. It's a huge hairy rat with a long tail. I feel like I'm going to faint."

"Zoe! Come help me! Hurry!" cries Lena.

I catch up to Lena.

"What's going on, Lena?"

"I lost Paco!"

"Who's Paco?"

Does Lena have a pet rat? Is that what she was petting in her bag earlier?

"Lena, did you really bring a rat with you?"

Lena gets wide-eyed with outrage.

"Are you crazy? Paco's not a rat. Paco's a chameleon!"

A chameleon! Yes, of course, a chameleon. A rat would have been unthinkable, but everyone walks around with a chameleon in their purse.

"Help me find him," Lena begs me, "poor Paco must be terrified, poor thing."

"Aah! Aaaaaaah!" Kim continues screaming, and her loyal followers, Angie and Clarisse, follow suit.

And suddenly in the midst of this chaos, the concerto for two mandolins by Vivaldi rises. My cell phone! I programmed my favorite music. I glance at the display. My parents, of course! I'm actually surprised at how long my mother has managed to wait to call me. I have no choice, but to answer. She'll just keep calling and calling until I pick up.

"Hello, Mom?"

I have to raise my voice to be heard over Kim's screams of terror and Lena's frantic calls for Paco.

"Is everything all right, darling? Everything going okay, I imagine."

That's my mother for you. This morning at the station, she was on the verge of tears as if I was leaving her for a world tour. Now, when everything is in chaos, she's cool as a cucumber.

"Yes, Mom, everything's okay."

"Have you made some new friends?"

"Zoe! Zoe!" Lena yells. "I see him. He's under the radiator! Come help me!" Lena calls urgently.

"Uh . . . I'm coming, Lena, I'm coming. Yes, Mom, I made friends," I say, heading toward Lena and the radiator.

"And, Vic? Everything going okay for her, too?"

I throw a glance toward Vic. Her arms are folded as she watches the chaotic scene unfolding before her eyes.

"Uh . . . yes, Mom, Vic is doing fine too."

"That's awesome to hear," exclaims my mother, who is always trying to sound cool and hip. "I'll make you a delicious dinner as a reward. What train are you taking home?"

"Mom, I don't know if I'll be coming home tonight yet. You know, I explained the rules to you."

"Zoe!" Lena shouts again.

Lena looks like she's about to lose her mind.

Kim is shouting for help as if the sky's falling!

"Yes, yes, I remember, sweetie. You said you might need to stay a few days if you were accepted. So! Have you been accepted, honey?"

"Not quite, Mom, but things are going well. Look, I've got to go know, they're calling me."

And with that, I quickly hang up. My mother means well, but she has a gift for putting me on edge. I don't know why. I move toward Lena, pushing past the frantic Kim who's gesturing wildly toward the radiator.

I kneel down and peek under the radiator to see

the source of all the trouble. First, I see two bulbous eyes that appear to be spinning in all directions at once. I better ask Lena if it's safe before I reach out to this creature.

"Does it bite?"

"Of course not," Lena sighs, "Poor little Paco does not bite. He's just a tame little pet."

"Paco," I say sweetly, "Paco, would you like to come out?"

"Zoe, if you can coax him out, I'll stand here and block his path in case he tries to run again."

Lena knows her pet well. I barely get my hand under the radiator when Paco bolts. Lena can't quite grab the chameleon, who skitters across the slippery floor right into Kim's expensive shoes.

"Help! Help!" Kim yells, grabbing at her foot. "It bit me. That monster bit me."

Lena scoops Paco up and the little reptile seems to snuggle up to her, if you can believe it.

"What is happening here?" a voice asks.

Everyone turns toward the door as it opens. Then Khan appears. He holds a sheet in his hand, and he raises eyebrows as he gazes at the scene before him.

Shared Dreams

Suddenly, everybody stops in their tracks.

"What is this mess?" asks Khan, taking in the over-turned chairs and students on the floor.

"And what on earth is that?" he asks, noticing Paco in Lena's arms.

"It's a chameleon, sir." Lena says in a tiny voice.

"You realize, sir," Kim immediately declares, "this animal is violent. He attacked me and tried to bite me!"

By this point, a knot of students are clustered around Lena and Paco. Even Vic is nearby. Suddenly a growling sound comes from Paco.

"It's his stomach. He's hungry," mumbles Lena without daring to look at Khan.

She pulls a jar out of her pocket, opens it, and takes something small and light brown in her hand.

I feel Vic start. She loves animals of all kinds, but she cannot tolerate bugs and insects. Paco, on the other hand, is delighted and quickly devours the snack.

"This has to be a health violation," Kim says. "Mr. Khan, are you going to let this girl get away with this? She should be dismissed from this audition."

Khan is frowning. Everyone has their eyes fixed on him. Lena's future is in his hands. He coughs. We listen and wait.

"It is true that animals are not allowed in our school," Khan begins.

This can't be happening. Will Lena's pet really get her expelled from Groove High before she even knows she's been accepted?

Suddenly, Tom takes a step forward. He looks Khan in the eye.

"This isn't Lena's fault, sir. I asked her to bring the chameleon in. I thought it would bring me good luck."

I look at Tom with round eyes. What is he saying? He's known Lena for two hours and he's sticking his neck out for her.

And I am even more surprised when I hear Vic speak up next. Vic—who just a little while ago was so jealous of Lena for making friends with me.

Vic pipes up, "No, it's my fault, Mr. Khan. I suggested Lena bring her pet to the audition for a joke. I thought it would be funny."

I can't believe my ears! Tom and Vic are standing up for Lena. I should say something, too.

"Yes, I was in on it, too. I thought it would be nice to have a pet to relax us at the audition," I add clumsily.

Khan looks at us one at a time, his black eyes flashing.

"I see," he says.

"There!" says Kim triumphantly. "You must deny all of them entry to this school!"

"Actually," Khan continues, "I'm going to let it pass for now. It's been a long day. Auditions can be nerve-wracking. And I think that's what we should focus on right now. Please put the pet away."

Lena breathes a sigh of relief. Me too, for that

matter.

"And," Khan continues, "please make sure I do not see this animal again."

Lena nods vigorously.

"Of course, sir!"

"Okay, now on to more important matters," Khan says, waving the sheet of names in his hand.

I hold my breath. With all the commotion, I had completely forgotten what today is really all about—our dreams, our futures.

"First," begins Khan, "those who are not accepted after today's audition should not be discouraged. You should continue to work hard, and come back to audition again next year."

That statement does it. All my fear and insecurity come rushing back. This is it. This is the fateful moment. A hand slides into mine. Vic.

Khan reads names: "The following students have been accepted to Groove High: Miss Kimberly Vandenberg. Miss Cindy Roberts. Miss Victoria Solis."

Vic! Vic has been accepted!

I squeeze Vic's hand back and whisper, "Congratulations, Vic!"

Meanwhile, Khan continues reading names.

"Miss Angie Brown. Miss Zoe Myer."

Zoe! He said "Zoe." My heart skips a beat. I've been accepted! I've been accepted to Groove High.

Khan continues, "Mr. Thomas Muller. Miss Lena Robertson."

It's a miracle. Suddenly, Tom, Lena, Vic, and I are in a big group hug. We're laughing and crying at the same time. Nearby, a girl stands motionless with tears rolling down her cheeks. Her name has not been called. I pause in my celebrating to wonder what I can say to comfort her, but I know there aren't any words. And I know that could just as easily be me in her place.

Vic takes me by the shoulders and looks me in the eyes.

"You know what we did today, Zoe?" she asks.

"What?"

"We started making our dreams come true!" Vic exclaims, shaking my shoulders.

And she's right. It may sound melodramatic, but she's right. We practiced so hard since we were little girls, taking ballet classes together for years. Always hoping we'd be accepted at a professional dance school, and now it has happened.

"I . . . I'm sorry about before," Vic begins, "I think I was a little jealous because you kept talking with Lena and . . ."

I interrupt her. "No, Vic, I should be the one apologizing. I missed your audition. I wasn't there for you."

"But I was being mean, Zoe."

"And I was being selfish, Vic. I promise it won't happen again . . ."

"Hey girls . . ."

We look up to see Lena, smiling.

"I'm the one who should be thanking everybody here. You all saved me by sticking up for me with the Paco disaster."

Okay, enough of this mush. Khan has reached the last name on his list, and he's trying to get our attention.

"Please know that Iris Berrens and I are very pleased to welcome you to Groove High. We have high hopes for all of you. I will now assign you to your rooms so you can settle in. At six o'clock, Miss Nakamura, Dean of Students, and Jeremy, the school supervisor, will come to introduce themselves."

Vic looks up to me and lets out a short, nervous

breath.

"Oh, there could be a big, big problem, Zoe . . ."

"What?"

"What if we end up sharing a room with that awful Kim?" Vic whispers.

"I hadn't even thought of that." But that is just one dark cloud hovering over this moment of victory.

"We'll have to see what happens, Vic."

Chapter 11

Welcome to Groove High!

I am now settling down in my new room. While the other girls compete for precious closet space, I pull out my journal and try to record everything that's happened in this crazy day.

You can read my first entry. "My new roommates, happily, are Vic and Lena (and Paco the chameleon, I suppose). Thank goodness, we are not stuck with Kim."

I think Kim's room is nearby. I thought I overheard her ordering Angie and Clarisse to go out and buy her sushi. Lena is trying to find a hiding place for Paco, since she really doesn't want to give him up. Vic tries not to grumble. She is positively disgusted by the dried locusts Lena feeds the chameleon, but everyone's trying to be supportive.

There's a quiet knock at the door. Vic opens it and

finds Tom standing outside.

"What are you doing here?"

"Quick, let me in," Tom whispers. "I'm not supposed to be in the girls' dorm, and if I get caught . . . "

Vic sighs, but allows him to come in.

Tom plops down on Vic's bed. Vic's eyes flash as he rumples the comforter she has just taken great pains to smooth out.

"You know what, ladies?" he says, "Since there were not enough boys in the first year, I am rooming with Luke Vandenberg!"

Vic's eyes grow larger.

"You're Luke's roommate?" Vic murmurs in disbelief.

"The very one," Tom says. "The brother of you-know-who." Then he jumps up and starts doing an imitation of Kim, ordering her followers around for sushi. His imitation really conjures up the queen herself, and Vic, Lena, and I burst out laughing. Tom really does great impersonations. Encouraged by our laughter, he offers another.

"Here, guess who this is."

He stiffens his back and frowns:

"Young people, you must give everything for this

school! You will need to work twenty-four-seven to keep up at Groove High. You will . . . "

"Iris Berrens," we shout out as a chorus before Tom says another word.

Suddenly Vic remembers something more serious. "Does anyone know about Edward Kauffman?" she asks suddenly. "Did he get accepted even after his fainting spell?"

"Yes, we talked about it back at the boys dormitory," Tom says. "He was accepted."

Before Tom can add any more information about the mysterious Edward Kauffman, Lena exclaims:

"Where is Paco?"

And here we are again, on all fours searching for Lena's chameleon. Once the chameleon is back in Lena's arms, I start interrogating Tom about Edward Kauffman. I want to learn all I can about my idol's mystery son.

There are so many things I want to learn about the world of dance, now that we're all students at Groove High. I have a feeling this is going to be a very exciting year!

Here is the west wing, with offices on the first floor; on the second floor are the boys' dorms.

The small park is for yoga classes or a place to relax after class.

Miss Nakamura's office. Note the view of the courtyard: escape is impossible!

The room that Tom, Luke, and Zach share.

The central building, with large dance halls, the main cafeteria, and the private apartments of permanent teachers (Mrs. Berrens, Khan).

Basketball courts and soccer fields. You can find Lena there!

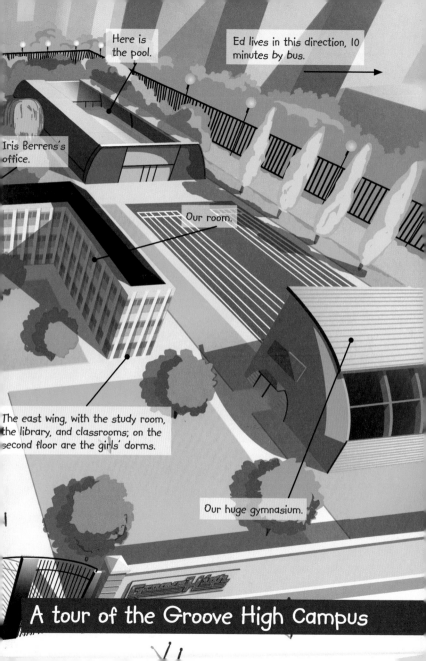

Our Dorm Room

Fashionably designed, well-lit, and well thought-out! Here's a small tour of the room . . .

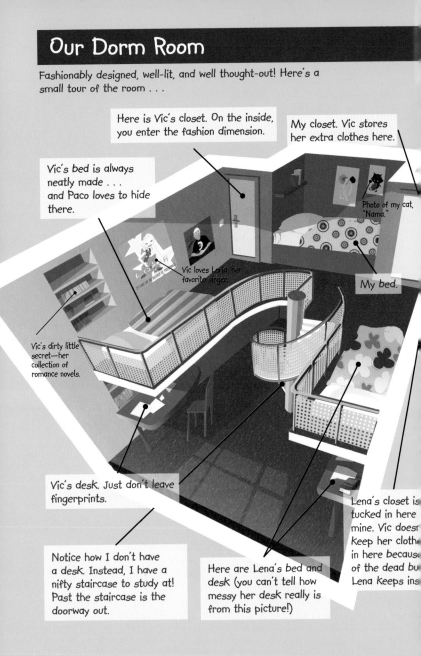

Here is Vic's closet. On the inside, you enter the fashion dimension.

My closet. Vic stores her extra clothes here.

Vic's bed is always neatly made . . . and Paco loves to hide there.

Photo of my cat, "Nama."

Vic loves Loria, her favorite singer.

My bed.

Vic's dirty little secret—her collection of romance novels.

Vic's desk. Just don't leave fingerprints.

Lena's closet is tucked in here mine. Vic doesn keep her cloth in here becaus of the dead bu Lena keeps ins

Notice how I don't have a desk. Instead, I have a nifty staircase to study at! Past the staircase is the doorway out.

Here are Lena's bed and desk (you can't tell how messy her desk really is from this picture!)

About the Author

Amélie Sarn: Amélie has two major flaws: excessive curiosity and a tendency to gorge herself. Not just on food, but on reading, travel, games, children, friends, and anything that makes her laugh. This gives her lots of material for stories! When her publisher asked her to write the stories of Zoe and the Groove Team, she revealed her dark side. Of all the characters in *Groove High*, she admits that her favorite is Kim!

About the Illustrator

Virgile Trouillot: With his feet on the ground, but his head forever in the clouds, Virgile spent his youth under the constant influence of cartoons, manga, and other comics.

When he's not illustrating *Groove High* Books, Virgile develops animated series for *Planet Nemo*. Virgile spends time in his own version of a city zoo that's right in his apartment. His non-human companions include an army of ninja chinchillas that he has raised himself and many insects that science has not yet identified.

Web Sites

In order to ensure the safety and currency of recommended Internet links, Windmill maintains and updates an online list of sites. To access links to learn more about the *Groove High* characters and their adventures, please go to www.windmillbooks.com/weblinks and select this book's title.

For more great fiction and nonfiction, go to www.windmillbooks.com.